ADVENTURE QUEST

THE TOWER OF MELGOTH

Book 1: Adventure Quest

Matt Whelan

ARROWCROFT PRESS

Cover design by: Ricky Gunawan

ISBN (paperback): 978-1-8384751-0-9

ISBN (ebook): 978-1-8384751-1-6

Published by Arrowcroft Press

This book is dedicated to my son Xander, the very first adventurer to defeat Melgoth, and my most enthusiastic supporter.

PREFACE

Welcome adventurer! This is your first step into a dangerous world of dragons, battles, sword-fighting and magic.

In each story, there are multiple ways to complete the quest. If you finish the adventure, feel free to go back and complete it a different way.
The choice is YOURS.

Each book contains a main quest and, for the mighty, a bonus quest. Can you complete both?

Be brave adventurer, the challenge lies ahead!

INTRODUCTION

You are Kylan Rett, a bold adventurer from the Kingdom of Vos. You have been chosen, by the King of Vos himself, to stop the evil wizard Melgoth, who is planning to unleash forces of darkness on all the lands by opening the Shadow Portal.

While trying to break into Melgoth's dark tower, you were captured by his soldiers and locked in the deep dungeons below. Melgoth has instructed the soldiers to keep you alive; he wishes to see you for himself.

If you are to survive and save the realm, you must escape from your cell, find your way out of the dungeons and locate the dark tower. Once there, you must confront Melgoth and destroy him before he can open the Shadow Portal.

Are you ready to take on this quest?

If yes, go to **[1]**

If not, close the book.

[1]

You wake up on the floor of a dark, dirty cell. Iron bars, and a locked, heavy gate, separate you from the corridor outside. Two soldiers guard the corridor. One is carrying a double-handed war hammer and pacing up and down, looking bored. The other soldier is fast asleep and snoring in his chair right outside your cell. He has propped his sword up against the wall by his feet.

The soldier with the war hammer scratches his beard and turns to the sleeping soldier.

"Oi! Wake up, you idiot!" he says, kicking his chair. "I'm going up top to get some fresh air. It stinks down here."

The sleeping soldier stirs and wakes up. The other soldier props his war hammer against the wall and walks out of a door at one end of the corridor, whistling a tune to himself as he leaves. The sitting soldier coughs, splutters, and closes his eyes. Within seconds, he is snoring again.

The old, scrawny prisoner in the cell next to you whispers, "Psst! Hey, you. Come here. Quickly."

You walk over to him. He puts his hand through the bars and gives you a metal tool.

"Take this," he whispers. "I am too old and weak to escape from this dungeon, but you are young and strong! You can get out of here and stop Melgoth."

You thank him and take the tool.

"You must go now. Quickly, before the other guard comes back."

If you want to use the tool to break out of the cell, go to **[20]**

If you want to wait for a better time to try to escape, go to **[35]**

[2]

Glad to have help, you stay with the archers. The leader introduces himself as Galen.

"That will not be much use here," he says, nodding towards your weapon. He hands you a spare bow and a quiver of arrows. You take the bow and arrow and hide your weapon in the tree, so no one else will find it.

Together with the group, you fire arrows at the soldiers on the other side of the river. The archers from Vos are skilful and have an excellent aim. Occasionally, an arrow from the other side slams into the trees you are using as cover.

You hold your breath, draw back the string, and lean out to the side. You see a soldier, take aim and release the arrow. The arrow soars across the river and strikes the soldier in the chest.

"Good shot, Kylan," says one of the women.

After ten minutes, you defeat the soldiers on the other side of the river. The survivors have run away. Melgoth will surely know that you are coming soon.

"Now is our chance," says Galen. "We must take the boat across."

You and the other archers follow Galen towards the boat. You all pile on board and Galen cuts the rope holding the boat in place. Two of the archers take up the oars and begin rowing across the river. On the other side, you and the group get out of the boat and drag it onto the shore.

Ahead of you, the tower looms. There are large marble steps which run up to an enormous front door. Galen puts a hand on your shoulder.

"This is Melda, Benn and Selma," he says, pointing to the others. "Allow me to introduce you properly."

If you want to be introduced to the others, go to **[42]**

If you want to carry on without being introduced, go to **[23]**

[3]

You climb the long marble steps with Galen. There are so many of them that you are both panting with tiredness when you reach the top.

The huge entrance doors to the tower loom above your heads. You wonder how on earth you will get in when, suddenly, the large doors swing inwards on their own.

Galen looks at you with concern, but then walks into the tower. It doesn't seem right that it should be this easy. You sense a trap.

You arrive in a grand entrance hall, lit by torches on the walls.

There are two stone stairways on either side, which both lead to the same door at the top. It doesn't seem to matter which stairway you take.

You and Galen take a step forward. The stone slab beneath you sinks into the ground under the pressure of your feet. From somewhere above, you hear a clicking sound.

If you want to wait and see what happens, go to **[22]**

If you want to leap away from the stone slab you have just pressed, go to **[43]**

[4]

You head left down the corridor, open the door which the other soldier went through and creep inside the room. The room is dark and your footsteps echo. From the light cast by a torch on the wall, you can just about make out some stone shelves built into the walls. On each shelf are old rags covering bones. You are in a crypt.

With a shudder, you make your way amongst the skeletons and look for another way out. Suddenly, there is a rustling sound.

To your horror, you find a skeleton on the lower shelf is

moving. The rags covering the bones fall to the floor and, with a clacking of bones, the skeleton stands up. It turns its skull towards you and approaches.

If you picked up the sword, go to **[8]**

If you picked up the war hammer, go to **[19]**

[5]

You and Galen ascend the staircase and eventually make it to a set of large double doors.

"Melgoth's throne room," says Galen, looking at the doors.

A noise from the other end of the corridor makes you and Galen jump; you both get an arrow ready in your bows. You take aim but then Melda, Benn and Selma come running down the corridor.

"Thank heavens you are okay!" shouts Galen.

"It wasn't easy getting here, but we made it," says Selma, smiling.

"Perhaps I was wrong, Galen," says Melda. "We should have come through the front door as you suggested."

You tell Melda that your route was also filled with danger.

Go to **[10]**

[6]

You drop back into the sewer. You are weary of the tentacled creature in the water and cannot really remember which way you came.

You wander the sewer endlessly until you become so tired that you have to sit down.

Another tentacle emerges from the water and wraps itself around your leg. You slice it off, as you did before, but yet another one comes.

A third tentacle grips hold of your sword hand; it squeezes so tightly that you drop the sword and are pulled into the slimy, foul-smelling water.

<u>Your adventure ends here.</u>

[7]

You set to work on the lock from the outside. The tool makes a loud noise as it scrapes against the metal. The soldier grunts in his sleep behind you.

"What are you doing?" whispers the old man angrily. "I am too old to go with you; leave me here."

You tell the old man you will not leave without him and keep scraping on the lock.

"Stop it, I beg you... look, behind you, he's waking up."

You turn around to find the soldier has woken up. He stands up quickly and dives at you before you can reach your weapon. He is big and strong and wrestles you to the ground. You try to struggle as he drags you back into your cell and slams the heavy door shut.

Your adventure ends here.

[8]

The skeleton walks up to you with surprising speed. You raise your sword and, as it comes closer, you stab and strike.

The sword clatters against the ribcage of the skeleton but does not hurt it. The skeleton grabs hold of you and pushes you into the wall. It is strong. You grapple and struggle against the skeleton, but it is no use, it does not seem to get tired. You try again with your sword, but the skeleton yanks it out of your hand and throws it away, out of reach.

The fight with the skeleton makes so much noise that the soldier who left returns and enters the room with two other guards, both carrying war hammers. They use their weapons to smash the skeleton into pieces. It is now just a pile of bones on the floor and is no longer moving.

With no weapon to defend yourself, they place you under arrest and throw you back in your cell, where you stay for the rest of your days.

<u>Your adventure ends here.</u>

[9]

Unable to see anything but darkness in the well, you lean further down for a better look.

Suddenly, the edge of the stone crumbles and huge chunks of the well fall down the dark shaft. You try to pull yourself back up, but it is too late. The side of the well collapses and you tumble down into the dark shaft. Everything goes black.

Your adventure ends here.

[10]

This is it. The throne room of Melgoth. The success of your quest depends on what happens next.

If you defeat Melgoth, you will save the Kingdom of Vos.

If you fail, Melgoth will open the Shadow Portal and summon an army of horrendous dark creatures, who will swarm across the lands.

"Kylan, this is your quest," says Galen. "You must face Melgoth and defeat him for the sake of the kingdom. Take one of us with you. The rest of us will stay outside these doors and defend you from any soldiers who try to come in."

If you want to take Galen with you, go to **[33]**

If you want to take Selma with you, go to **[38]**

If you want to take Melda with you, go to **[39]**

If you want to take Benn with you, go to **[44]**

If you want to face Melgoth alone, go to **[48]**

If you want everyone to come with you and leave the door undefended, go to **[49]**

[11]

Making as little noise as possible, you and Galen head left down the corridor as you search for a staircase going upwards. You walk through a series of corridors until eventually it opens out into a large room. There is a door on the opposite side of the room.

In the centre of the room is a huge, mean-looking ogre. He is ugly and covered in iron plates of armour strapped to his yellowish muscles. In his left hand is a large iron shield the size of a dining table. In his right hand is the biggest hammer you have ever seen in your life.

He is facing the other way and does not know that you are watching.

If you would like to attack the ogre, go to **[36]**

If you would like to go back the way you came and check out the other end of the corridor, go to **[45]**

[12]

Disgusted by the smell of the sewer, you head back the way you came and navigate the maze of corridors. You eventually recognise the door to the cell block you were being kept in. You open it slowly and poke your head in.

This was a mistake; the other soldier has come back and woken up his friend. They see your head pop through the door and give chase. You run down the corridor, but your pursuers are shouting loudly. More guards emerge from the other doors.

There are too many for you to fight and win. They escort you back to your cell, where you spend the rest of your days.

Your adventure ends here.

[13]

Melda draws her bow and nocks an arrow. You do the same. You both release your arrows at the same time. The ogre is big and hard to miss but the arrows bounce harmlessly off his armour.

You realise that, with your bow and small dagger, you do not stand a chance against such a fearsome enemy.

He rushes at you with surprising speed and raises his huge hammer. As he smashes it down on the ground, the shock waves knock you and Melda down. He raises the hammer a second time and slams it down hard. Everything goes black.

<u>Your adventure ends here.</u>

[14]

The tentacle pulls you towards the water. It is strong. You try to pull your leg back, but it keeps yanking you closer.

As the creature in the water prepares for another pull, you raise the sword and chop down at the tentacle.

You hear a shrill squeal from beneath the slimy water and see more bubbles on the surface. You chop again and slice right the way through. The stub of the tentacle goes back under the water.

The piece still attached to your leg falls off and stops moving. Before the creature can strike again, you run towards the ladder and haul yourself up. You throw open the hatch and climb out into another room.

There is one door in and out of the room.

If you want to walk through the door, go to **[16]**

If you want to head back into the sewer, go to **[6]**

[15]

The soldier regains his balance but, as he does, you step towards him. You are now so close that he cannot swing his sword at you. As he runs into you, you bend down so that he falls over your back. As he topples over, you stand up and give him a deliberate shove towards the window.

The window smashes as the soldier goes through it, screaming all the way down. With a splosh, he lands in the river. You continue to stare until eventually his head pops up and you see him swimming frantically to get to the shore. Melda looks at you and smiles.

"That was close," she says. "If we make it through this, I will give you some archery lessons."

You both continue down the corridor where you eventually find some steps going upwards and head towards the throne room.

As you reach the huge, oak double doors to the throne room, you hear a commotion from the opposite side of the corridor. There is a clattering of swords and a soldier drops to the ground. Benn, Galen and Selma come running around the corner and meet up with you and Melda.

"Nice of you to join us," says Melda calmly, a small smile on her lips.

Benn nods and Selma grins.

"Only just," admits Galen. "Perhaps we should have gone your way after all."

Go to **[10]**

[16]

You open the door and the fresh air hits you. You hold your hand up to your face to shield your eyes from the natural light, which you haven't seen since they captured you.

Beyond the door is an open field. The large grey walls of the dungeon are behind you. At the other end of the field there is a river and beyond it you see the dark Tower of Melgoth. It is a huge, thick tower with strange stonework jutting out here and there. It looms high into the sky. Every stone block and iron-framed window speaks of great evil.

You can hear a lot of noise and shouting and spot a group of archers wearing clothes which look like those worn by the Vos Army. They are hiding behind some broad trees; the river is just beyond them. A small rowing boat is tied to a post on the riverbank.

On the other side of the river, you see enemy soldiers, dressed just like the ones you have escaped from. They have bows and arrows too.

You run as quickly as you can towards your fellow countrymen. There are two men and two women in the group. You reach the trees. An arrow from across the river whizzes by, nearly hitting you in the head. You try to introduce yourself to the group.

"We know who you are, Kylan," says a man with brown hair. He has a sword at his belt and appears to be the leader.

"The king has sent us to rescue you," says one of the women.

You thank them for coming to help you, but tell them you must defeat Melgoth before you can escape.

"Then we are at your service," says the leader. "Allow us to help you."

If you want to stay with the group of archers, go to **[2]**

If you want to proceed alone and make your way to the boat on the river, go to **[31]**

[17]

You tell Galen that you believe that Benn's idea of getting into the tower via the storage room is the way to go.

Galen thinks for a moment and says, "Very well, you and Benn go together. The rest of us will go through the front door."

He removes a dagger concealed in his boot and hands it to you.

"Here, just in case," he says.

With that Melda, Galen and Selma climb the steps to the tower.

"This way," says Benn.

You follow Benn around the side of the tower where there is a small stone building which joins onto the main tower. There is a horse-drawn cart full of barrels and boxes. There is a line of soldiers moving the goods from the cart into the storage area.

"There's too many of them. We need to create a distraction," says Benn.

If you want to create a distraction, go to **[27]**

If you disagree with Benn and want to sneak past the soldiers, go to **[24]**

[18]

Quietly, you both head left down the corridor, looking for a staircase going upwards. Eventually the corridor turns a corner. Melda peeps around and quickly snaps her head back.

"There are three guards, armed with swords," she reports. "How is your aim with a bow?"

If you would like to attack the three guards, go to **[28]**

If you would like to see what is at the other end of the corridor, go to **[29]**

[19]

The skeleton walks up to you with surprising speed. You raise your war hammer and, as it comes closer, you slam it down hard. With a crunch of bones, the hammer smashes the skeleton's arm clean off its shoulder. Even so, the skeleton keeps on coming.

You continue to strike with the heavy war hammer and, with each blow, another piece of the skeleton breaks off. Eventually, the skeleton is just a pile of bones scattered across the floor. It is no longer moving.

You see a door at the end of the crypt, but you can hear voices from the other side of it. It must be the soldier returning from the surface. It sounds like he now has even more men with him.

If you want to fight the soldiers, go to **[34]**

If you want to hide somewhere in the crypt, go to **[41]**

[20]

You go to work on the lock with the metal tool, and eventually it springs open. The sleeping soldier does not wake up. It would be sensible to take one of the weapons which the soldiers have left propped up against the wall.

Will you take the **sword** or the **war hammer?**

Remember your choice.

You pick up the weapon and feel its weight in your hands; it is heavy and well crafted.

There are two ways to leave the corridor: at the end of the corridor on the left, where the other guard went, or the door at the end of the corridor on the right.

If you want to exit the corridor through the door on the left, go to **[4]**

If you want to exit the corridor through the door on the right, go to **[47]**

If you want to go to the cell next to yours to help the old man escape, go to **[26]**

[21]

Holding your breath, you lift the grate up on its hinges and look down into the sewer.

In the middle there is a slow-moving river of foul-smelling water. On either side are two ledges, just wide enough to walk on. Avoiding the water, you drop onto one ledge and sidestep through the sewer.

The sewer twists and turns for a long time. The smell makes your stomach heave and you are glad that it has been a while since you last ate.

Eventually, you turn a corner and see a ladder leading to a hatch at the top. You make your way towards it, but suddenly something bubbles in the foul water by your feet.

A large green tentacle emerges from the bubbles and wraps itself around your ankle. You feel it tugging you towards the slimy water.

If earlier you picked up the sword, go to **[14]**

If earlier you picked up the war hammer, go to **[40]**

[22]

Galen looks down at the stone slab which has moved and then up to hear where the clicking sound is coming from. Suddenly, there is a loud clang and spiky iron bars shoot up from the ground and form a square around you. The gaps between the bars are too tight to squeeze through. You are trapped.

All at once, the stone slabs that you and Galen are standing on slide apart, revealing a long drop down the dark shaft below.

You both try to climb up the iron bars, but they are too slippery and you keep sliding back down. The stone slabs have now disappeared, revealing only the shaft. You and Galen, having nowhere to place your feet, slide down and drop into the darkness below.

Eventually, the slide ends and you come crashing to a stop in a cramped stone room. There is no way in and no way out. In the small amount of light, which is coming from the top of the shaft, you can see the skeletons of former adventurers who have also fallen down here, covered in cobwebs and dust.

There is no escape from this trap.

<u>Your adventure ends here.</u>

[23]

"Right, let's climb the steps and see if we can get in through the front door," says Galen.

"With respect, Galen, I believe the front way is too obvious and will be heavily guarded," says Melda. "Let's go around the tower and climb up; we can get inside through one of the upper windows."

"You're both wrong," says Benn in his deep, gruff voice. "There is a storage room around the side; we can enter the tower through there."

Galen turns to you and asks, "What do *you* think, Kylan?"

If you agree with Galen and wish to go through the front door, go to **[3]**

If you agree with Melda and wish to climb through the upper windows, go to **[25]**

If you agree with Benn and wish to access the tower via the storage room, go to **[17]**

[24]

You and Benn creep from behind your hiding spot and make it to the corner of the wall. You wait for a soldier to climb into the cart and then slip inside the storage room.

You both hide behind a stack of boxes, but there are lots of soldiers and very few places to hide. The soldier who went into the cart comes back out carrying a box and spots you both.

"Hey!" he shouts. "Over there!" He drops the box and draws his sword. All the other soldiers draw their swords too. There are seven of them in total.

You cannot possibly win this fight. Benn knows this and drops his sword to the ground, raising his hands in surrender. The soldiers throw you both in jail, where you spend the rest of your days.

Your adventure ends here.

[25]

You tell Galen that you agree with Melda and think that climbing through an upper window is the best course of action.

Galen thinks for a moment and then says, "Very well, you and Melda climb the tower and find a way in." He turns to Benn and Selma. "The rest of us will try through the main door." He crouches down and pulls out a dagger, hidden in his boot, and hands it to you.

"Just in case," he says, giving you a nod. With that he, Benn and Selma start the long, hard journey up the stone steps.

"Let's go, there's not much time," Melda says to you and runs around the tower.

Melda's footsteps are almost silent as she runs around the side of the tower. She is quick on her feet and it is difficult to keep up with her.

She reaches a place that is out of sight and climbs the tower, using small holes and gaps in the stonework. She is an excellent climber, and you attempt to follow her exactly, using the same holes and ledges as she does.

Eventually you both reach a ledge by a window on the fourth floor. Melda slides open the window and pokes her head in.

She turns to you and says, "It's all clear, let's go."

You both hop in and find yourselves in an empty corridor. It is clean, unlike those in the dungeons. There are pictures on the walls.

"Which way?" asks Melda. "We need to find the top floor of the tower; that's where Melgoth's throne room is."

There is nothing notably different at either end of the corridor.

If you would like to go left down the corridor, go to **[18]**

If you would like to go right down the corridor, go to **[29]**

[26]

You creep to the cell next to you and start working on the lock from the outside, being careful not to wake the sleeping soldier.

The old man raises a hand and whispers, "Thank you, my son, but I am too weak to escape from here. You must go alone." He looks you directly in the eyes. "You *must* defeat Melgoth, the entire realm depends on it! But beware, my boy; he is a powerful wizard, and you cannot defeat him with just that weapon. Lean closer to me…"

You lean in to listen to what the old man has to say, despite his awful smell.

"The only way to defeat Melgoth is to turn his own dragon against him. He keeps his dragon close by in his throne room. His dragon obeys him, but only because she is under his spell. Break that spell and she will turn on her master. Now go!"

If you want to exit the corridor through the door on the left, go to **[4]**

If you want to exit the corridor through the door on the right, go to **[47]**

If you want to break the old man out of the cell anyway, go to **[7]**

[27]

You tell Benn to wait there while you handle the distraction. You creep towards the cart and slip underneath. No one sees you.

You draw your dagger and use the point to loosen the screws which fix the wheels to the cart. Once the wheels are barely hanging on, you wait until no one is looking, roll back out from under the cart and sneak back to where Benn is waiting.

You both watch nervously as a soldier climbs up onto the cart to get another barrel. His weight makes the cart wobble and the wheels you have loosened come flying off. The cart tips over, scattering barrels and boxes in all directions. Some barrels burst, spilling their contents onto the floor.

All the soldiers from the storeroom run out panicking; two of them slip on the spilled liquid and fall over. There is an argument between the soldiers about whose fault the mess is.

This is your chance. You and Benn slip past the distracted guards and make your way into the tower.

You walk up some spiral stairs and reach another floor. There is another set of stairs going upwards, but the way is barred by a locked gate.

If you want to go exploring the rest of this level, go to **[46]**

If you want to break the lock and make your way upstairs, go to **[37]**

[28]

Melda draws her bow and nocks an arrow in place. You do the same. She gives you a nod and together you jump around the corner.

Melda releases her arrow and, before you can even take aim, she fires another one. Both of her arrows hit their targets and two guards drop to the ground. You aim for the third one and fire, but you have taken too long, and the guard dodges your arrow.

He is now running at you with his sword drawn. Melda fires a third arrow, but it bounces off his metal helmet. It knocks him off balance but he keeps running. He is now stumbling towards you, sword raised.

If you want to escape, go to **[32]**

If you want to use the fact that the guard is off balance to your advantage, go to **[15]**

[29]

Making as little noise as possible, you both head right down the corridor as you search for a staircase going upwards. You walk through a series of corridors until eventually it opens out into a large room.

There is a door on the opposite side of the room. In the centre of the large room is a huge, mean-looking ogre. He is ugly and covered in iron plates of armour strapped to his yellowish muscles. In his left hand is an iron shield the size of a dining table. In his right hand is the biggest hammer you have ever seen in your life.

He is facing the other way and does not know that you are watching.

If you would like to attack the ogre, go to **[13]**

If you would like to go back the way you came and check out the other end of the corridor, go to **[18]**

[30]

You put down the hammer and lift yourself onto the edge of the well. Cool air hits your face as you stick your head down the well shaft. There is no way of telling how deep it is. There does not appear to be a rope, ladder, nor any handholds.

You notice the well is old and badly built. Loose stones crunch under your weight and some fall down to the bottom. It is a long time before you hear a splash.

If you want to lean closer to have a better look, go to **[9]**

If you want to go back and walk out of the door, go to **[16]**

[31]

You thank the archers but tell them you must face this danger alone.

"Then that is the way it shall be," says the leader. "Good luck, Kylan. You will need it if you are to face Melgoth alone."

He bows and then takes his place with the group, who continue to fire arrows at the enemy soldiers across the river.

You run towards the boat. Arrows whoosh overhead from both sides. You sidestep as an arrow sails close by.

Eventually you reach the boat but the archers on the other side of the river see you. You cannot escape. The last thing you see is a hail of arrows coming down upon you.

Your adventure ends here.

[32]

"Run!" you shout to Melda. She turns away from the soldier and runs. He slashes at you with his sword, narrowly missing you, and stumbles into the wall.

You and Melda run down the maze of corridors, with the soldier hot on your heels.

Eventually, you reach a large chamber. In the centre of the room is a huge, mean-looking ogre. He is ugly and covered in iron plates of armour strapped to his yellowish muscles. In his left hand is an iron shield the size of a dining table. In his right hand is the biggest hammer you have ever seen in your life.

The guard behind you is shouting. The ogre turns to look at you and raises his hammer to strike. You are now trapped between the guard and the ogre. You cannot defeat both.

Your adventure ends here.

[33]

You open the door to the throne room and walk in with Galen. The throne room is big and grand. At the very end, Melgoth sits on a black throne. His skin is grey and cracked and his eyes are black and filled with malice. Across his lap is a long staff with a glowing red orb on the end. To the right of the throne is the frame of the Shadow Portal, which has not yet been activated.

Curled around the throne is an enormous red dragon, with a fierce face and scaly, armoured skin. She hisses as you approach and goes to stand up, but Melgoth holds out his hand and says, "Stay,

my beauty," and the dragon lies back down. "Let's see what these adventurers have to say."

"It's over, Melgoth!" shouts Galen.

Melgoth replies by letting out a deep, evil laugh which echoes around the throne room.

"You puny humans are no match for my powers."

"We will see about that," declares Galen, who begins running towards the dark wizard.

Melgoth picks up his staff from across his lap and fires a green blast of energy, which covers Galen and glows brightly. When the green light fades away, nothing is left of Galen but dust, which floats gently to the ground.

While he is distracted, you fire an arrow at Melgoth. It hits him in the arm. He yells in pain and drops his staff, but the red dragon stands up and breathes her fiery breath on you. As the flames get closer, you realise there is nothing you can do to protect yourself.

<u>Your adventure ends here.</u>

[34]

The door opens and two armed guards, plus the soldier who was outside your cell, walk into the crypt.

"Him!" shouts the soldier, pointing. "He's escaped. Stop him!" The other guards raise their war hammers. You put up a good fight, but you cannot take on three guards at once.

The guards overpower you and the guard whose war hammer you stole takes it back from you.

They throw you back into your cell, where you spend the rest of your days.

Your adventure ends here.

[35]

You wait and wait. Eventually the other soldier comes back. A better opportunity to escape does not arrive. The soldiers do not feed you; you get hungry and weak and spend the rest of your brief life locked in the prison cell.

Your adventure ends here.

[36]

You and Galen step out from the shadows and nock arrows into your bows. The ogre sees you and grunts. You both fire your arrows, but they ping off the ogre's armour. You immediately regret your decision to attack this gigantic monster. The ogre charges at you and Galen. Each of his footsteps rocks the ground.

Galen throws down his bow and draws his sword, standing bravely in the way of the huge ogre running towards him. With a swing of his giant hammer, the ogre swats Galen away like a fly and sends him crashing into a wall. The ogre turns his attention to you. You look at Galen, who is lying, perfectly still, on the ground. You fire another shot with your bow; this one sticks in a gap between the ogre's armour but all it is does is make him angrier.

He roars in pain and charges at you. You try to run away, but he is surprisingly fast for a creature so big. You look over your shoulder and see him gaining on you, raising his hammer to strike.

You run as fast as you can but suddenly, with a thump, everything goes black.

<u>Your adventure ends here.</u>

[37]

You try to pick the lock with the metal tool the old man gave you, but this lock is heavier and it doesn't work.

"Stand back," says Benn. He draws his two-handed sword and, with one clean strike, smashes the lock off the gate. His strength impresses you.

The two of you head up many sets of spiral stairs. You eventually come to the top floor of the tower. This must be where Melgoth's throne room is.

You head around a corridor and spot Galen, Melda and Selma waiting outside a pair of oak double doors. You run to meet up with the three of them.

Go to **[10]**

[38]

You open the door to the throne room and walk in with Selma. The throne room is big and grand. At the very end, Melgoth sits on a black throne. His skin is grey and cracked and his eyes are black and filled with malice. Across his lap is a long staff with a glowing red orb on the end. To the right of the throne is the frame of the Shadow Portal, which has not yet been activated.

Curled around the throne is an enormous red dragon, with a fierce face and scaly, armoured skin. She hisses as you approach and goes to stand up, but Melgoth holds out his hand and says, "Stay,

my beauty," and the dragon lies back down. "Let's see what these adventurers have to say."

Selma throws back her hood, revealing her bright red hair.

"You should be careful keeping a dragon as a pet, Melgoth," she says calmly. "They can be very dangerous."

"This dragon is under my spell," barks Melgoth. "She does as I command. Allow me to demonstrate her power."

Melgoth turns to the dragon but, before he can speak, Selma says, "No, allow me to demonstrate *mine*."

Without warning, Selma raises her staff and chants strange

magical words. A light emerges from the red crystal in her staff and shines on the dragon. The dragon grunts and shakes her head.

Selma seems to connect with the dragon and smiles kindly. "Yes, you are free now," she says.

"No, stop that!" shouts Melgoth, sounding worried. He turns to the dragon. "Kill them both, you horrible beast!"

But the dragon is looking at Melgoth and grumbling loudly.

Melgoth raises his staff to the dragon, but it is too late. She rears her head and engulfs Melgoth in flames before he can cast his spell.

When the flames subside, there is nothing left of Melgoth but a pile of ash on the black throne.

The dragon turns to you and Selma. For a moment, you worry you will both share Melgoth's fate, but Selma walks confidently to the dragon and puts a caring hand on her enormous face.

"It is okay," she says soothingly. "Go now and be with your own kind."

The dragon screeches loudly and, with a swing of her mighty tail, smashes the Shadow Portal into pieces. She flaps her enormous wings and bursts through the throne room windows, taking out sizeable chunks of the wall as she does so.

You and Selma walk to the tremendous gap in the wall and watch as the dragon soars into the distance.

Galen, Benn and Melda join you in the throne room.

"You're both alive!" Galen says.

"What about the guards?" Selma asks.

"They too were under Melgoth's spell. When you destroyed him, the spell broke. They stopped fighting us and ran away."

"We are victorious!" shouts Benn, clapping his huge hand on your shoulder.

Melda simply smiles.

To claim your victory, go to **[50]**

If you want to take on a bonus quest, go to **[51]**

[39]

You open the door to the throne room and walk in with Melda. The throne room is big and grand. At the very end, Melgoth sits on a black throne. His skin is grey and cracked and his eyes are black and filled with malice. Across his lap is a long staff with a glowing red orb on the end. To the right of the throne is the frame of the Shadow Portal, which has not yet been activated.

Curled around the throne is an enormous red dragon, with a fierce face and scaly, armoured skin. She hisses as you approach and goes to stand up, but Melgoth holds out his hand and says, "Stay,

my beauty," and the dragon lies back down. "Let's see what these adventurers have to say."

Melda says nothing but draws her bow in a flash and fires an arrow at Melgoth. You do the same.

But Melgoth is expecting this. He raises his right hand, and a red shield of energy surrounds him. The arrows bounce off the shield and clatter onto the floor.

Laughing, Melgoth turns to his dragon and says, "Now!"

The dragon rears her head towards Melda, her great nostrils filled with flame. You run at Melda and try to knock her out of the way, but you are too late. You feel the searing heat of the flames as they surround you both and everything goes white.

Your adventure ends here.

[40]

The tentacle pulls you towards the water. It is strong. You try to pull your leg back, but it keeps yanking you closer.

You swing at the tentacle with the war hammer, but it is a hard weapon to use in the cramped sewer. You bash the tentacle with the head of the hammer, but it is no use.

The tentacle pulls with all its might and drags you into the slimy, foul-smelling water. You are never seen again.

Your adventure ends here.

[41]

Hearing the voices coming nearer you dive onto the now empty shelf and hide under the rags where the skeleton came from. The door opens and two guards, plus the soldier who was guarding your cell, walk into the crypt talking and laughing.

They walk right past your hiding spot.

"Wait!" one of the guards shouts. The other men stop talking. Your heart stops and you breathe in, trying to be perfectly still in the silence.

"What is this mess?" asks another. You realise they are talking about the skeleton bones all over the floor.

"Just leave it," says another. "The caretaker will clean this up later."

Kicking a few bones aside, the guards carry on talking and laughing and then continue towards the cell block.

Knowing you won't have long before they realise you have escaped, you emerge from the rags and run through the door, taking the war hammer with you.

You go through a series of doors until you find stairs going up. You can feel the cooler air as you climb higher.

Eventually, you come to a small room. In the centre of the room is an old, stone well. Beyond the well is a wooden door.

If you want to go through the door, go to **[16]**

If you want to explore the well, go to **[30]**

[42]

Galen points to the lady on the left. She has brown hair, which is mostly hidden beneath the hood of her cloak.

"This is Melda; she is our best archer," he says. "She doesn't say much, but she can hit a target from a hundred yards with her eyes closed."

Melda nods to you.

Galen points to the man in the middle and says, "This is Benn; he is the best fighter amongst us."

Benn is big and strong, has long blond hair tied in a ponytail and a large double-handed sword slung over his muscular back.

"Good to meet you, Kylan," he says in a deep voice.

Galen points to the last member of the group, a woman with striking red hair. Across her back is a staff with a glowing red crystal in the top.

"This is Selma, our magician. She studies magical creatures."

"Greetings," she says to you. You notice a dragon brooch on the hem of her robes.

You tell them it is good to meet them and they offer you a slight bow in return.

Go to **[23]**

[43]

Something is very wrong, but you don't know what it is. With your quick reflexes, you grab Galen by the shoulder and pull him away from the stone slab. You both fall over and land in a heap on the floor.

Galen is angry with you and shouts, "What are you–" but, before he can say any more, spiky iron bars shoot out from the floor and form a square around where you had just been standing.

The floor slabs within the square of iron bars move apart with the sound of grinding stone. Beneath the slabs is an enormous drop down a dark shaft. You do not know what is down there, but it certainly would not have been good. It appears Melgoth had set you a trap which you almost fell into.

"Thank you, Kylan," says Galen, still shocked. "You've saved us both."

Suddenly, a voice booms around the entrance hall, although there is no one else in there. It seems to come from the stones themselves.

"So… you avoided my trap?" The voice is calm but evil, and the mere sound of it makes your skin crawl. "Fear not; there are plenty more on the way and, if you get past those, you will still have to face me!"

With that, manic laughter fills the hall and then fades away to nothing.

"Melgoth," says Galen. "Let's go. His throne room is on the top floor."

You both run up the staircase and through the door at the top. There is a corridor which goes in both directions.

If you wish to go left down the corridor, go to **[11]**

If you wish to go right down the corridor, go to **[45]**

[44]

You open the door to the throne room and walk in with Benn. The throne room is big and grand. At the very end, Melgoth sits on a black throne. His skin is grey and cracked and his eyes are black and filled with malice. Across his lap is a long staff with a glowing red orb on the end. To the right of the throne is the frame of the Shadow Portal, which has not yet been activated.

Curled around the throne is an enormous red dragon, with a fierce face and scaly, armoured skin. She hisses as you approach and goes to stand up, but Melgoth holds out his hand and says, "Stay,

my beauty," and the dragon lies back down. "Let's see what these adventurers have to say."

"You have tormented our lands long enough!" shouts Benn. "This ends here!"

Melgoth curls his lips into a cruel grin and says, "For you, perhaps."

Benn charges towards the throne, giving his loudest battle cry.

Melgoth picks up the staff from across his lap and fires a green blast of energy, which covers Benn and glows brightly. When the green light fades away, nothing is left of Benn but dust, which sprinkles to the ground.

While Melgoth is distracted, you fire an arrow at him. It hits him in the arm. He yells in pain and drops his staff, but the red dragon stands up and breathes her fiery breath on you. As the flames get closer, you realise there is nothing you can do to protect yourself.

Your adventure ends here.

[45]

After sneaking past guards through a maze of corridors, you eventually reach a staircase going up. A sign on the wall says THRONE ROOM and there is an arrow pointing upwards.

If you want to go up the stairs, go to **[5]**

If you want to go back and explore the other end of the corridor you started at, go to **[11]**

[46]

You leave the locked gate and begin searching the rest of the level you are on. The throne room is on one of the higher levels of the tower, but you cannot find another set of stairs. All you find are locked doors and stairs going back down.

About half an hour passes as you creep past guards and look for another way up to the throne room.

Eventually Benn says, "Perhaps we had better go back to the locked gate. I am sure I could smash the lock off with this." He pats the hilt of his double-handed sword.

You agree and set off but, suddenly, a loud and evil voice booms throughout the tower. It sounds like the voice is coming from the walls themselves.

"It would appear we have two intruders in our midst," the evil voice declares.

Benn looks at you, his eyes wide. "Melgoth!" he declares.

"I have captured your friends who I found outside my throne room and it won't be long before I capture you too. Guards! Find them at once and bring them to me!"

The evil voice of Melgoth laughs and the sound slowly fades away.

Soldiers emerge from all the locked doors, looking for you both.

You run through the corridors trying to find your way to the gate, but eventually the soldiers find you. There are too many of them. You throw down your weapons and are escorted to the throne room to meet your doom.

Your adventure ends here.

[47]

You open the door at the end of the corridor and walk through. It leads to a series of other corridors. You try to open a few doors, but they are all locked.

Eventually, you reach a foul-smelling room which is unlocked. There are no other doors out of this room. In the centre of the room there is a large grate on the floor. Below the grate is an even smellier sewer.

If you want to go back the way you came and try the other door at the end of the corridor, go to **[12]**

If you want to open the grate and drop into the smelly sewer, go to **[21]**

[48]

You open the door to the throne room and walk in alone. The throne room is big and grand. At the very end, Melgoth sits on a black throne. His skin is grey and cracked and his eyes are black and filled with malice. Across his lap is a long staff with a glowing red orb on the end. To the right of the throne is the frame of the Shadow Portal, which has not yet been activated.

Curled around the throne is an enormous red dragon, with a fierce face and scaly, armoured skin. She hisses as you approach and goes to stand up, but Melgoth holds out his hand and says, "Stay,

my beauty," and the dragon lies back down. "Let's see what this adventurer has to say."

You tell Melgoth that his reign of terror is over and that you have come to end his plans to bring darkness to the world.

Melgoth chuckles. "You dare to face *me*, alone? You are very brave or very stupid, my boy."

You draw your bow and fire an arrow at Melgoth. He is expecting this and produces a red energy shield around him. The arrow hits the energy shield and falls to the ground.

"Is that it?" scoffs Melgoth. "You should have brought your friends with you."

He picks up his staff and points it towards you.

"Now, prepare to experience true power."

A green bolt of energy emerges from the staff straight towards you. It is too fast to dodge. You do not know what kind of spell he has cast on you, but the green light is the last thing you ever see.

<u>Your adventure ends here.</u>

[49]

You tell Galen that you must all fight together to defeat Melgoth.

"But Kylan, we will be exposed from behind if we all go in there."

You insist that this is the only way to defeat him.

"As you wish," says Galen, shaking his head. "Let's go together."

You open the door to the throne room and walk in with Galen, Melda, Selma and Benn. The throne room is big and grand. At the very end, Melgoth sits on a black throne. His skin is grey and cracked and his eyes are black and filled with malice. Across his lap is a long staff with a glowing red orb on the end. To the right of the throne is the frame of the Shadow Portal, which has not yet been activated.

Curled around the throne is an enormous red dragon, with a fierce face and scaly, armoured skin. She hisses as you approach and goes to stand up, but Melgoth holds out his hand and says, "Stay, my beauty," and the dragon lies back down. "Let's see what these adventurers have to say."

"It's over, Melgoth!" shouts Galen.

Melgoth replies by letting out a deep, evil laugh which echoes around the throne room.

"You puny humans are no match for my powers."

"We will see about that," declares Galen, who begins running towards Melgoth. Benn goes running with him. Selma has her staff in both hands and begins uttering a chant. Melda draws and fires an arrow. You do the same, but not as fast.

Melgoth stands and raises his staff. An energy field surrounds him and the arrows bounce harmlessly off it.

The dragon rears her head and fires a blast of flame, which covers Galen and Benn. When the flames fade away, there is nothing left of Benn and Galen but ashes.

The dragon turns to you and Selma; the beast's great nostrils fill with flames as she prepares to breathe another fiery blast. Selma raises her staff.

"NO!" she shouts in a commanding voice.

The dragon stops for a second and cocks her head to one side.

"What are you doing, you stupid creature?" bellows Melgoth. "Destroy them!"

The dragon looks uncertain. You think that Selma may have broken the spell on the dragon, but then the double doors behind you open suddenly and five soldiers walk into the room behind you. They grab Selma.

Melgoth points his staff at you and fires a green blast of energy. This is the last thing you ever see.

<u>Your adventure ends here.</u>

[50]

You have done it!

You have defeated the evil Melgoth and brought peace and happiness to the Kingdom of Vos.

After saying goodbye to your new friends, you return home, where you receive a hero's welcome from your people.

You have an audience with Theldred, the King of Vos, who gives you a golden sword and shield as a reward. He gives you the title *Defender of The Realm* and offers you a chest full of gold coins as payment for your great deed.

You and your family move to a large house, close to the Royal Palace, and spend the rest of your days in happiness and peace.

THE END

[51 – BONUS QUEST]

You all walk down the long marble steps and gather at the bottom. As you are about to say your farewells, a deafening screech makes you look upwards.

The dragon you set free is circling in the sky and shrieking. The others duck, as if threatened, but Selma raises her staff. Red light shines from the crystal in the top.

The dragon swoops down and, with a beat of her huge wings making air rush past your face, she lands heavily on the ground. Her head thrashes around at the end of her long neck.

"Is it in pain?" asks Galen.

"She," Selma corrects, "and yes. But she is not injured." Selma walks over to the dragon and places her hand carefully on the creature's scaly head, making some kind of magical mind link.

Selma says nothing for a moment, and then her face becomes sad.

"It is her family," Selma says. "She has two young children. Melgoth took her away from them, and she does not know how to get back home. She doesn't know where she is."

The dragon lets out a low moan of despair. You find it hard to believe that you feel such pity for a creature so fearsome.

You ask Selma where dragons come from.

"This one, I believe, is a Nyrnian Broadtail. They come from the Mountains of Nyrn, many leagues from here, and beyond the Alderrat Foothills to the north."

Selma slings her staff over her back and fixes it in a loop on her robes. She turns to the group.

"Go home and celebrate our victory over Melgoth. I must help this dragon find her way home."

If you want to go with Selma to help the dragon find her home, go to **[65]**

If you want to return home and claim your victory, go to **[50]**

[52]

You tell Selma to instruct the dragon to attack the camp, but only target the wooden structures. You tell her you don't want the captured dragons or anyone in the tents to be harmed.

Selma puts a hand on the dragon's neck and silently gives her instructions. The dragon swoops swiftly downwards and hovers above the camp. She breathes her fiery breath on one of the wooden structures, and it splinters and breaks apart with the heat and power of the blaze.

With another blast of flame, she destroys the other wooden

structure. The dragon then lands next to the two chained dragons and, using her strong tail, rips the stakes that attach the chains out of the ground. The other dragons are now free.

The dragon trappers emerge from their tents. The sight of their camp on fire greets them. They soon notice that the two dragons they have captured are no longer chained to the ground.

You tell Selma that this would be a good time to leave. She agrees. The dragon launches upwards, leaving the smoking camp behind.

Selma is beaming when she turns to you and says, "Ha! That serves those horrible dragon hunters right."

You continue flying over the plains until the land below you becomes lush and hilly, with winding rivers and deep valleys.

Without warning the dragon groans, drops through the air slightly and recovers herself. You and Selma jump at the sudden fall.

"She is weak and tired," Selma says. "Melgoth mistreated her. We *must* stop for a rest."

If you want to insist that the dragon keeps flying, go to **[56]**

If you agree with Selma and want to land so that the dragon can rest, go to **[60]**

[53]

You tell Selma that you do not have time to waste and have to keep on going.

"With respect, Kylan," she says, "I don't think she can take much more. She is exhausted."

As if understanding the conversation, the dragon lurches in mid-flight again and lets out a low groan.

If you want to insist that the dragon keeps flying, go to **[56]**

If you agree with Selma and want to land so that the dragon can rest, go to **[60]**

[54]

Selma gives a silent instruction to the dragon, who flies directly towards the gathering dark clouds.

Together, you fly straight into the storm. All around you is nothing but grey. Thunder rumbles. The harsh wind and rain whips at your faces.

"We can't stay in this!" Selma shouts over the noise. "Should we fly below the clouds or above them?"

If you want to drop below the clouds, go to **[61]**

If you want to fly above the clouds, go to **[67]**

[55]

You head into the forest, walking as quietly as a mouse. You search for some time, but do not come across any other animal. Just as you are thinking you made a mistake coming into the forest, you hear a rustling sound from behind you.

You turn around and spot, through the trees, a deer who is grazing on the red berries of a bush. The deer has not noticed you.

Carefully you unsling your bow from your back and nock an arrow. Slowly and quietly, you draw back the bowstring. You take a deep breath, just as your father taught you, until the bow is perfectly still, and then release the arrow.

You strike the deer and run over to collect it. You lift it across your shoulders and head back to Selma.

On your way back, you spot something unusual on the ground. It looks like a piece of rope, hidden under a pile of leaves. The leaves did not get into a pile like that on their own; someone has put them there.

If you want to investigate the rope and the leaves, go to **[59]**

If you want to head back to Selma with the deer, go to **[63]**

[56]

You insist the dragon must keep going. Selma scowls at you, then puts her hands on the dragon's neck.

"I'm sorry," she says quietly, "but you have to fly a little further."

The dragon groans and then beats its wings harder. You fly for several minutes over the Alderrat Foothills.

Suddenly, the dragon emits a piercing shriek and then begins to fall. Totally exhausted, the dragon has passed out.

Selma desperately tries to revive her, but it is no use. You have pushed the dragon too far.

The dragon tumbles to the ground with you and Selma still on her back.

<u>Your adventure ends here.</u>

[57]

Before the farmers can get too close, you run for it. You have always been a fast runner, but the weight of the sheep on your back slows you down.

You risk a look over your shoulder and see that two of the farmers are chasing, but the other one is loading a stone onto a sling.

You continue to run and suddenly something strikes at your lower back. The pain is intense and makes you stumble, but you keep running.

Another pain, this time in the back of your head. You crash to the floor. Your eyes go blurry.

You wake up to find that it is night time. You have a splitting headache. You find that the dead sheep has gone, as have all your weapons.

You try to find Selma and the dragon, but you can't find your way in the dark. You never see either of them again.

Your adventure ends here.

[58]

You walk inside the cave with Selma. The dragon's head peers inside and she makes a strange clicking sound.

Suddenly, two young dragons come bursting out from within the cave and begin flapping their wings and jumping up at their mother. You are very glad you agreed to help Selma with this quest.

When the young dragons settle down, they come over to you and begin sniffing at you. They are very curious and allow you to stroke them. After a while, Selma goes over to the mother dragon and puts her hand on the creature's head once more. She stays there for quite a while and then smiles and turns to you.

"She says we must stay here tonight and rest. Tomorrow she will take us close to the nearest town, and from there we can make our way back to Vos."

You agree with the plan.

"She also said that she and her young owe us a life-debt. For the rest of their lives, if either of us is ever in trouble, we can call for their help, wherever we are. They will know if we are in trouble and they will come."

With no other options apart from the hard, stone floor of the cave, you and Selma sleep with the young dragons in their nest made of twigs and branches.

You wake up in the morning, thinking that was possibly the worst night's sleep you have ever had, but then you remember Melgoth's dungeons!

As promised, the dragon drops you and Selma off at a little town called Rensbrook in the Alderrat Foothills.

From there you take a ship across the Naryth Ocean and, after many days at sea, return to the Kingdom of Vos.

Go to **[70]**

[59]

You approach the pile of leaves and the exposed piece of rope. You take another step and suddenly feel something snag around your ankle. There is a whirring sound and a heavy barrel tied to the rope falls from the branches above.

As it falls, you are heaved upwards. The dead deer falls from your shoulders and you are left hanging upside down by your ankle. The rope around your ankle is digging in painfully.

You remove the dagger from its sheath on your belt and begin sawing through the rope.

Eventually it gives and you fall downwards. You land head first on a rock. Everything goes black.

Your adventure ends here.

[60]

The dragon lands in a small valley on the pebbled shore of a large lake. You and Selma jump off the dragon's back and stand and watch her. She shuffles along on her belly, clearly exhausted, and edges closer to the lake.

When her head is close enough, she laps up the water with her tongue and, after a few gulps, collapses completely on the ground. Selma runs over to her and places a hand on her scaly side.

"She's breathing," Selma announces, "but she is very weak. We need to get her some food, quickly. I don't think she can hunt for herself."

You ask Selma what dragons eat.

"Meat," she replies. "Any animals they can find, really. I am sure we can find something for her in these parts. I'll stay and protect her. Do you think you could go and hunt for something?"

You look around. There is a small forest to the east and some open fields to the west. You could probably find animals to hunt at either location.

If you want to head east to the forest, go to **[55]**

If you want to head west to the open fields, go to **[66]**

[61]

The dragon swoops down, searching for a way out of the clouds. A flash of lightning illuminates the clouds and is followed, almost instantly, by a deep roll of thunder.

Lower and lower the dragon swoops, but the grey clouds seem endless. Suddenly another flash of lightning erupts, and this time it strikes the dragon.

Without a sound, the dragon goes limp. Its head dangles low and its wings stop beating.

"Wake up!" Selma shouts to the dragon, but it is no use.

Together, all three of you go tumbling towards the ground.

<u>Your adventure ends here.</u>

[62]

You apologise to the farmers and explain that you were out hunting (although you do not mention that you are trying to feed a dragon) and that you did not know the sheep belonged to them.

"Be that as it may, lad," the oldest farmer says, "we can't let you take something that belongs to us."

You offer your sword as payment, assuring them it is good-quality steel. You convince them that the sword is worth more silver coins than their sheep.

The farmers consider this for a moment and look at one another, then the eldest says, "Aye lad. We accept."

You unbuckle Galen's sword from your belt and throw it over to the farmers.

"Peace be with you," one of them says to you. The other tips the brim of his hat to you.

You walk off back the way you came.

Go to **[63]**

[63]

You return with the spoils of your hunting and set the dead animal down in front of Selma.

"Very good," she says. "This will do nicely." Selma raises her staff and points it at the dead animal. "You may want to step back a little," she adds.

You take a step back. The red crystal at the top of the staff glows and flames dance around it. A small blast erupts and the animal you hunted is set on fire.

After two minutes, Selma uses her staff to draw the flames back in. The dead animal is now cooked. The smell of the cooked meat reminds you that you also have eaten nothing since you were captured.

Just as you consider going to eat some meat, the dragon wakes up from her slumber, sniffing the air. She immediately spots the food you have left for her, gobbles the whole animal up in one gulp and then goes back to sleep.

You and Selma look at each other for a moment and then erupt into laughter.

While you let the dragon rest, Selma goes foraging in the forest and returns with some berries and nuts, which you both eat greedily, followed by a drink from the fresh water of the lake.

After a couple of hours, the dragon wakes up. She walks over to you both and nuzzles her head against Selma, then against you.

Selma laughs and says, "You're definitely feeling better, aren't you?"

You are happy to see the dragon has recovered. You pat her on the head and tell Selma that it is time to finish the job.

You both climb onto the dragon's back and take off once more. You fly for some time over the Alderrat Foothills until they grow into the base of Nyrn Mountains. The dragon screeches excitedly.

"She knows where she is now," Selma says. "She knows the way home."

The dragon soars high over the Nyrn Mountains. The scenery is breathtaking. Eventually, the dragon lands on a ridge high up in the mountain range. The ridge leads to an enormous cave mouth. The dragon gestures with her head for you to go inside.

Go to **[58]**

[64]

You tell Selma that you do not wish to attack the camp because you do not want to harm anyone.

"But they are dragon trappers," Selma replies. "If we leave them alone, they will follow us." Selma points down below. "Those large wooden towers are net launchers. If we destroy them quickly, it will keep the trappers busy. Nobody will get hurt, but they won't be able to fire at any passing dragons."

If you want to target just the wooden structures, go to **[52]**

If you want to continue to avoid the camp, go to **[68]**

[65]

You tell Selma that you will stay with her and help the dragon find her family. You bid farewell to the others.

"Here, take this," Galen says, unbuckling his sword belt. "You will need it more than I will."

You thank Galen and strap on his sword belt. Selma touches the dragon's head once more.

After a moment she turns to you and says, "I have told her we will help her get home. She will allow us to ride on her."

Riding on top of a dragon does not feel like the safest way to travel, but you have made a promise to Selma.

You both climb onto the dragon's back, Selma in front. The beast's scaly body is not as hard as it appears, but she is still uncomfortable to sit on. With a huge beat of her wings, she takes off.

You wave to the others but, in no time at all, they look like small dots down below.

"The most direct route to the Nyrn Mountains is that way, but it looks like there's a storm gathering," Selma says, pointing to ominous-looking clouds. "We could fly through the storm, or try going around it and over the Blasted Plains. The weather is fairer that way, but there are many dragon trappers who live in the Plains."

If you want to fly directly into the storm, go to **[54]**

If you want to go around the storm and over the Blasted Plains, go to **[69]**

[66]

You walk across the open fields in search of animals to hunt. You find a dirt track and follow it for an hour. Eventually, you come to a field with sheep grazing in it. This will have to do.

You take aim with your bow, loose an arrow, and collect the dead sheep, swinging it over your shoulders. As you head back towards the lake, three farmers approach you. One is carrying a pitchfork, and the other two have similarly dangerous-looking farming tools.

"Stop there, lad!" one of the men shouts.

"That sheep you've just killed belongs to us," says another.

You do not particularly want to fight these men; they are farmers, not soldiers, after all. But it is important you get back to the dragon before it is too late.

If you want to run away from the farmers, go to **[57]**

If you want to offer the farmers something in return, go to **[62]**

[67]

The dragon beats its enormous wings and you go higher and higher, although it all looks the same in the bleak greyness of the storm.

Lightning flashes nearby, lighting up the clouds. A few moments later, a deep rumble of thunder rolls past. Selma urges the dragon to fly higher still until eventually you break through the clouds into the blue skies above.

The dragon keeps flying, and finally the storm and darkness are behind you. The land ahead is lush and hilly, with winding rivers and deep valleys.

Without warning the dragon groans, drops through the air slightly and recovers herself. You and Selma jump at the sudden fall.

"She is weak and tired," Selma says. "Melgoth mistreated her. We *must* stop for a rest."

If you want Selma to urge the dragon to keep flying, go to **[53]**

If you agree with Selma and think the dragon should rest, go to **[60]**

[68]

You insist on continuing without attacking the camp and fly right over it.

For several minutes you continue over the vast, dry landscape of the Blasted Plains. A screech behind you makes you turn around.

The two blue dragons you saw before are flying behind you, each one mounted by a masked rider. Both dragons have metal contraptions over their mouths and chains in the hands of the riders. As they fly closer, you realise they are unfurling a large net.

"Dive down!" yells Selma, but it is too late. The dragon trappers are upon you and the net traps all three of you. Your dragon cannot beat its wings and you all tumble down towards the ground.

You survive the fall but spend the rest of your days in the captivity of the dragon trappers.

<u>Your adventure ends here.</u>

[69]

You tell Selma that the storm looks too dangerous and that you should fly around it. Selma silently tells the dragon this. The dragon swoops and heads eastwards, avoiding the clouds.

Together, you fly for over an hour. The ground below becomes flatter and dustier. The plants look tougher, the grass yellow.

"These are the Blasted Plains," Selma says. "Dangerous lands. There are dragon hunters everywhere. We must be careful."

You fly for some time until you spot a strange-looking camp down below. You can make out several horse-drawn carts, a few tents and two large wooden structures the likes of which you have never seen before. On the edge of the camp are two blue dragons, tied down with chains and stakes.

"Trappers!" shouts Selma. "Kylan, we have to destroy that camp."

If you want to attack the camp, go to **[52]**

If you want to ignore the camp and fly over it, go to **[64]**

[70]

You have done it!

You defeated the evil Melgoth and brought peace and happiness to the Kingdom of Vos. In doing so, you also reunited the dragon with her family and have made a lifelong magical bond with them.

You return home, where you receive a hero's welcome from your people.

You have an audience with Theldred, the King of Vos, who gives you a golden sword and shield as a reward. He gives you the title *Defender of The Realm* and offers you a chest full of gold coins as payment for your great deed.

You and your family move to a large house, close to the Royal Palace, and spend the rest of your days in happiness and peace.

THE END

CHARACTER PROFILES

Kylan Rett

Born in Valdur, the capital city of the Kingdom of Vos, Kylan is the son of a blacksmith and a weaver. Forever chasing adventure, Kylan has carried out many tasks in service of King Theldred. His quest to defeat Melgoth is his most dangerous yet.

Galen Crowe

The youngest soldier ever to be promoted to the rank of Captain, Galen has served in the Vos Army for five years. A natural leader, Galen is trained in the use of many weapons. King Theldred selected him to lead the mission to rescue Kylan from Melgoth's dungeons.

Melda Shadowleaf

Little is known about Melda's background, although rumour has it that she used to be a master burglar working, against her will, for the Thieves Guild in the City of Olberan. Her speed and stealth are only matched by her skill with a bow and arrow.

Benn Flint

Raised in the Galwick Highlands, Benn and his family had to flee from Melgoth's army who brought destruction on his village. Vowing to one day take revenge, Benn spent most of his childhood training as a warrior under the teachings of his uncle. When armed with his double-handed sword, few opponents can defeat him in combat.

Selma Altaani

Trained as a Fire Mage Acolyte in the Tower of Valdur, Selma soon discovered a passion for dragons and dedicated herself to the study of magical creatures under the guidance of the legendary Dragon Rider, Bhazen Threll.

EXCERPT FROM BOOK 2: *ESCAPE FROM BLACKROCK ISLAND*

You take one final step towards the edge of the plank and draw in a deep breath.

"Good riddance, ya scurvy sea dog," Hadwin growls at your back. "I wished we'd have done this years ago.

You turn your head slightly and tell Hadwin that he will regret this decision and that you will reclaim the *Silver Storm.*

"Ha!" he spits. "In two days from now, we'll be on Marley Island chugging back grog and YOU will be at the bottom of the Sea of Sorrows," he grins and a glint of sunlight reflects off his golden teeth. "If yer lucky."

Hadwin raises his cutlass and takes a step onto the plank. "Now get out of my sight or yer'll be jumping in with my sword in yer back."

You do not doubt that the man is serious. Summoning all of your bravery, you count to three and jump off the plank.

Splash!

The weather has been hot and thankfully the sea is not too cold. You swim up to the surface and watch as your ship, the *Silver Storm*, sails northwards. The crewmen lean over the deck and watch you trying to stay afloat. Some are laughing and pointing at you. Others just watch.

You remember from the sea charts nailed to the wall of your cabin that there is a cluster of islands to the south.

If you want to swim back towards the *Silver Storm* and ask the crew to take you back on-board, go to **[22]**

If you want to swim southward, go to **[41]**

STAY IN TOUCH

To be kept up to date about the release of future *Adventure Quest* books, please visit:

www.adventure-quest-books.com

Alternatively, please email any questions to:

news@adventure-quest-books.com

*

Social Media

Facebook:
@AdventureQuestBooks

Instagram:
@adventurequest.books

Twitter:
@AQBooks

ACKNOWLEDGEMENTS

There are many people who helped bring this book, and indeed this series, into being, but I would like to give special thanks to the following:

My wife, Rachael, who continually pushed for me to develop this book. Of all my projects, she truly believed in Adventure Quest from the very beginning.

My editor, Ian Howe, who miraculously makes the editing process one of my favourite parts of developing a book.

My cover designer, Ricky Gunawan, who completely blew my mind when he brought the characters to life with his amazing artwork.

Finally, to Lyn and Edward Oakes, who were the very first people, outside my family, to read the book. I will never forget how positive I felt after reading their feedback, which was both constructive and encouraging.

Thank you all.

ABOUT THE AUTHOR

Matt Whelan grew up near Chester, North West England.

At the age of ten, his father handed him a copy of The Lord of the Rings, which he spent the next two years reading (with the help of a dictionary). This kicked off a long-lasting love of the fantasy genre.

Wanting to share this passion with his own children, he created an interactive fantasy adventure which was accessible to his six-year-old son and hence Adventure Quest was born.

When not writing, he can be found spending time with his wife and two young children or throwing a ball for his dog Neo.